SUPER HAPPY PARTY BEARS

KNOCK
KNOCK
on
WOOD

KNOCK KNOCK on WOOD

MARCIE COLLEEN

[Imprint]
MAKE YOUR MARK

NEW YORK

[Imprint]
MAKE YOUR MARK

A part of Macmillan Children's Publishing Group

Super Happy Party Bears: Knock Knock on Wood.
Copyright © 2016 by Imprint. All rights reserved. Printed in China
by Toppan Leefung Printing Ltd., Dongguan City, Guangdong Province.
For information, address Imprint, 175 Fifth Avenue, New York, N.Y. 10010.

Library of Congress Cataloging-in-Publication Data is available.
ISBN 978-1-250-09808-5 (paperback) / ISBN 978-1-250-10675-9 (ebook)
Our books may be purchased in bulk for promotional, educational,
or business use. Please contact your local bookseller or the Macmillan
Corporate and Premium Sales Department at (800) 221-7945 ext. 5442
or by e-mail at MacmillanSpecialMarkets@macmillan.com.

Book design by Natalie C. Sousa
Imprint logo designed by Amanda Spielman
Illustrations by Steve James

First Edition—2016

1 3 5 7 9 10 8 6 4 2

mackids.com

TO BOWIE:
THANKS FOR THE INSPIRATION.

CHAPTER ONE

Welcome to the Grumpy Woods!

Well, not really. Just kidding. You may as well just turn around and go back. No one is welcome here. The rock wall should have made that clear.

It might not be a big wall, but it
makes its point. You see, there
used to be a tall wooden fence to
keep out certain folks—especially
bears. Especially bears who
like to dance and sing and make
doughnuts and have parties. But
then a bunch of beavers chewed it
down and used it for their dam. It's
kind of a sore point around here.

In fact, there is a new Mayoral Decree regarding beavers. Let me see your teeth—you aren't a beaver, are you? Beavers are no longer welcome in the Grumpy Woods. But that is a different story from a different book.

Of course, right now you might
be thinking, *Bears are cute* and
Parties are fun and *What's so bad
about beavers?* Cut it out. The
animals of the Grumpy Woods do
not agree, because every animal
here is, well, *grumpy*.

That upturned log in the center of the woods is City Hall. No, it's not really a hall. It's often confused with other upturned logs in the Grumpy Woods, which really irks Mayor Quill. So he ordered a brand-new sign to officially mark it. He's really proud of that sign.

Well, Mayor Quill
held a very official
meeting at City Hall.
Everyone—from Opal Owl to Dawn
Fawn—attended.

At that particular meeting, it
was decided that new measures
must be taken to keep
strangers out of the
Grumpy Woods. No
one wanted to take
any chances after the
Beaver Incident.

So even though all welcome signs, welcome mats, and mailboxes had already been removed, and the Welcome Wagon had been rolled off the Grumpy Cliff by an official decree of the mayor, the townscritters decided to take further action to keep the Grumpy Woods free of intruders.

Everyone voted. And that was that. It was very official.

Humphrey Hedgehog, assistant deputy to Mayor Quill, presented his blueprints for a new and improved Grumpy Fence. It wasn't so much a fence as a towering wall made of the heftiest rocks this side of the Grumpy River.

Construction started right away.

However, Bernice Bunny and Dawn Fawn struggled under the weight of the boulders.

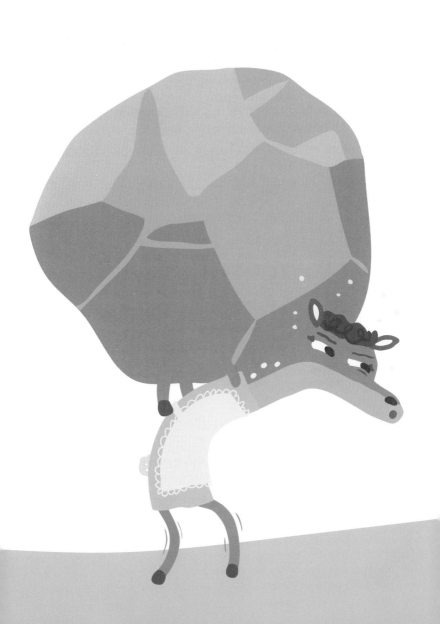

After only five minutes on the job,
Opal Owl went on strike, claiming
she was molting from the stress of
carrying such heavy rocks.

And one of the largest stones got away from Squirrelly Sam and rolled onto Sherry Snake. It took the entire crew to free her.

When it was finished, it wasn't towering at all. It wasn't really even much of a wall. It was more like a pile. So Humphrey made everyone gather a bunch of twigs to stick along the top of it.

It isn't a very impressive "fence." But don't say that to Humphrey.

He does not want to admit the
project was a disaster. He insists
that Sherry still patrol along the
fence twice a day.

And so, every day, everyone
in the Grumpy Woods wakes up
already needing a nap, takes a
quick ride on a mood swing, and
orders up some breakfast—two
hot cross buns and a bowlful of
Who cares!

That is, everyone except the
Super Happy Party Bears!

See the mailboxes dangling like
ornaments from the shrubbery?
And the welcome mats stacked like
a house of cards to create a cozy
canopy in front of
the main entrance?

That's the Party Patch, the

HEADQUARTERS OF FUN—

where the Super Happy Party Bears

have made their home. Life is very

different there. Life is super. Life is

happy. And life is full of parties!

If you follow the carefully placed

sticks, laid out in the shape of

arrows up the flower-lined path, you'll see the welcome sign out front. On top of the sign sits a little stick-figure diorama that includes the likeness of each Grumpy Woods neighbor. They are wearing party hats and dancing. The leader of the party appears to be Mayor Quill.

See, while the others in the Grumpy Woods can't stand the bears, the Super Happy Party Bears *adore* their neighbors, especially the mayor.

And so, on a beautiful morning such as this, the Super Happy Party Bears get up at YAY O'CLOCK, take a quick walk on sunshine, and order up some breakfast—a bowlful of awesome sauce and a short stack of *Hot Diggity Dogs!*

Nothing annoys the critters of the Grumpy Woods more.

Except when the bears have a party.

And they are always having a party.

2

CHAPTER TWO

Knock knock, knockity knock.

All morning long, a rhythmic tapping had been shaking every leaf and disturbing every critter in the Grumpy Woods. Humphrey the Hedgehog was on an official mission to put an end to the racket.

He couldn't be happier. It was his longtime dream to evict the Super Happy Party Bears from the Grumpy Woods once and for all. Because whoever got rid of the

possible culprits

1. The Super ~~EVICTED~~ Party Bears

2. Thirsty Birds

Super Happy Party Bears would be a hero. And everyone knows that heroes can have statues of themselves in parks and have holidays on their birthdays and, most important, become mayors.

Mayor Quill was a fine mayor. But, truthfully, Humphrey thought the porcupine was a bit of a softie sometimes. He required evidence before tossing the bears out. Well, this time the evidence could be heard echoing off the trees. *Knock knock, knockity knock.*

Mayor Quill had declared by order of Mayoral Decree 427 that knocking was not permitted in the

Grumpy Woods. No one really visited anyone else anyway, so knocking on doors was no longer necessary. But it was up to Humphrey to find out who was to blame for the noise. Humphrey was pretty sure he knew where to start.

As he turned up the path to the Party Patch, lined with cheerful flowers and arrows made of twigs pointing toward the welcoming door, Humphrey stumbled over one of the twigs.

"Harrumph!" Humphrey kicked *all* the twigs, causing them to scatter. "Try following *that* path!" he muttered as he trudged on.

Once at the door, Humphrey banged loudly to be heard over the commotion inside. Official mayoral business allowed for the breaking of Mayoral Decree 427.

"You need to say 'Knock knock,'" instructed a voice on the other side of the door.

"Knock. Knock," he repeated.

"Who's there?" sang out the voice on the other side.

"Humphrey Hedgehog, assistant deputy to the mayor, His Excellency. I am on—"

"Humphrey *who*?" interrupted the melodic voice.

"OPEN THIS DOOR AT ONCE!" yelled Humphrey.

"You didn't say 'please,'" the voice sang out. This was true. And Humphrey didn't see the harm in being polite.

"*Please* open this door," said Humphrey.

The door swung wide open, revealing a dance party of epic proportions.

"HUMPHREY!" the bears all cheered.

And before he could object, Humphrey was pulled into the Party Patch, where a party hat was slapped on his spines and a cup of apple juice was put into his paw.

"I'm actually here on very important official business," said Humphrey, trying desperately to be heard over the music.

"What?" asked the bears. "We can't hear you." They continued to dance to the strong thumping bass.

"Very. Important. Official.

Business," yelled Humphrey.

"ABOUT THE MUSIC!"

"Isn't it FABULOUS?" asked

Shades, peering over his star

glasses.

"It's the best music ever!"

exclaimed Mops as he flipped his

mop-top hair to the beat.

Even the bubbles Bubs was calmly blowing in the corner seemed to bounce in rhythm. In fact, the entire Party Patch was shaking with the music.

Humphrey marched over to the Super Happy Party Band and

grabbed the microphone out of Ziggy's paw, replacing it with his own cup of juice.

"WE LOVE KARAOKE!" cheered Ziggy.

"SUPER HAPPY KARAOKE TIME! SUPER HAPPY KARAOKE TIME!" the bears chanted, and did their Super Happy Party Dance.

Slide to the right.

Hop to the left.

Shimmy, shimmy, shake.

Strike a pose.

35

One by one, Humphrey snatched the instruments away from the band—Jigs's maracas, Little Puff's xylophone, and Flips's trumpet (which was really just an inventive way of using his party hat). Then, with a spiny hip-check, he sent Big

Puff sliding across the dance floor, away from his pots-and-pans drum set and straight into a conga line.

Yet even without the Super Happy Party Band, the beat went on. But how?

Humphrey was flabbergasted.

Just then the littlest bear tugged on Humphrey's sleeve.

"Would you care to sing a duet?" said the littlest bear, looking at the microphone still in Humphrey's paw.

"What in the world is causing that horrendous knocking?" asked Humphrey, dropping all the instruments to cover his ears.

"Not *what* in the *world*," said the littlest bear. "*Who* in the *trees*!" And he pointed out the window to a woodpecker pecking a beat into every darn tree in the woods.

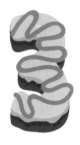

CHAPTER THREE

Humphrey stood at the bottom of a tree and looked up. Wallace Woodpecker was drumming with his beak, and by now it had given Humphrey a major headache.

"Excuse me," Humphrey called. "By order of the mayor, I am going

to have to ask you to stop that
noise this instant."

But Wallace could not hear
Humphrey.

Small flakes of bark drifted to the
ground like snowflakes as Wallace
pecked on. A few chips fell onto
Humphrey's nose, and he quickly
harrumphed them off.

Using Flips's party hat as a
megaphone, Humphrey tried
once more. "You, in the tree!
I need to ask you to stop that.
Immediately!"

The drumming stopped.

"I think he has a song request,"
explained the littlest bear.

"Oh, okay. I thought maybe
I did something wrong," said
Wallace, and he flew down to take
Humphrey's request.

"Actually, I'm here on official
business," said Humphrey. "You
have to stop drumming. By order of
the mayor."

"What did I do
wrong?" asked Wallace.

"NOTHING!" cheered the bears. Humphrey scowled.

"I'll ask the questions here," said Humphrey. "Firstly, who are you?"

"Wallace Woodpecker," Wallace answered.

"He's our *new* friend!" the bears quickly added, and cheered.

Humphrey stayed focused on his

interrogation and made notes on
his clipboard. "Where did you come
from, Wallace? I've never seen you
around the Grumpy Woods before."

"Oh, I just got here!" said
Wallace. "They invited me." He
pointed to the bears, who beamed
proudly at their feathered buddy.

"We were out for a stroll this

morning when we heard the most
magnificent drumming," explained
Mops.

"It was perfect for sunrise
dancercising," added Jacks.

"So we invited Wallace to share
his most excellent skills with the

rest of the
neighbors,"
continued
Big Puff.

"In hopes
that it would
bring us all together,"
said the littlest bear sweetly.

"And it did! Humphrey's here!"
the bears cheered.

"One last question: *How* did
you get over the Grumpy Fence?"
Humphrey was referring to his
personal magnum opus, the newest

piece of architecture in the Grumpy

Woods, designed to keep out all

intruders. As mentioned in Chapter

One, it was really just a small pile of rocks and twigs.

Wallace simply fluttered his wings. "I flew!"

Humphrey growled. Obviously they needed a taller fence.

"Well, I am going to have to cite you for disrupting the peace in the Grumpy Woods," scolded Humphrey. "And you do not have a permit to perform music in public. So you must stop this instant."

"What is a permit?" asked Mops.

49

"If you have to ask, you don't have one," snapped Humphrey.

"I'm so sorry," said Wallace, hanging his head in shame. "I was only trying to be a good neighbor."

"Good neighbors don't make noise," whispered Humphrey.

The bears gathered around to
comfort Wallace as Humphrey
turned on his heel and left. Only
one problem . . .

"How do you get out of this
place?" Humphrey called back to
the bears.

"Follow the twig arrows on the flower-lined path," they replied.

Humphrey looked down at the disheveled pile that *used* to be the twig arrows. How was he supposed to follow that? He spun around to complain, and his paw slipped on a loose twig.

Humphrey slid to the right. He hopped to the left. He wobbled on one foot, which caused him to shimmy and shake. And when he started to lose his balance, he quickly struck a pose. It all looked very familiar to the bears.

CHAPTER FOUR

"It's no use," sobbed Wallace as he flitted back up the trunk of the tree and gathered his belongings in his knapsack. "I'll never fit in anywhere!"

"Don't say that, Wallace," said the littlest bear. "You belong here with us."

"Birds of a feather stick together," proclaimed Bubs. He placed his party hat on his nose as if it were a beak. The bears *oooh*ed and slowly nodded in agreement.

"You don't understand," explained Wallace. "I've flown just about everywhere. But it's always the same. After a while, I am told

my pecking is too noisy and I'm kicked out. I'll never find a home."

"We LOVE your pecking!" cheered the bears.

"It makes me happy," added the littlest bear, giving his tush a little shake.

"But it made everyone else in the Grumpy Woods angry. I can't stay here now," said Wallace.

56

"Sure you can," said Big Puff. "All you have to do is show them hepcats there's more to you."

"There's nothing more to me," sobbed Wallace. "Nothing I do is good enough."

Just then, Flips looked at Wallace through his telescope (again, yet another use for his party hat) and spied something in the tree trunk behind him. Wallace's pecking had carved a beautiful design of swirls and curls into the bark.

"What is *that?*" asked Flips.

Wallace blushed and tried to hide the handiwork with his wings. "It's nothing. Just a little something I do. It's doodles mostly. Nothing special."

All the bears took turns viewing the masterpiece through Flips's telescope.

"IT'S BARK-TASTIC!" they all agreed.

However, Wallace explained that no one had a need for such woodworking. He had been all over, and no matter where he went, he was told to leave the trees alone.

"Sounds like you've been pecking up the *wrong* trees," said Mops.

"We have plenty of trees here

in the Grumpy Woods," said Little

Puff. "Well, we *did* have lots of

trees, before the beavers used

them to build their lodge. But more

are growing in."

"I'm not welcome here," said

Wallace. "You heard that angry

fellow with the spikes."

Wallace had a point. Humphrey had said that Wallace must stop drumming by order of the mayor. That sounded pretty official.

"Well, if you have to leave," said Ziggy, "let's at least play you some Super Happy exit music."

The Super Happy Party Band gathered their instruments from

the pile that Humphrey had dropped them in.

"One problem," said Jigs. "My maracas broke." She held up the sad pair of busted shakers.

"No worries," said Ziggy. "We can find a substitute."

"SEARCH PARTY!" cheered the bears as they looked for stand-in

maracas. They tested every pinecone, leaf, and small stone, but nothing seemed to work—until . . .

"Here ya go," said Wallace, handing Jigs two perfectly whittled wooden maracas. Little seeds rattled inside. The handles had been carved with care and a note was attached to one of them.

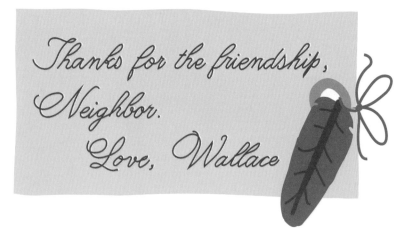

Thanks for the friendship, Neighbor.
Love, Wallace

"You made these?" asked Jigs, admiring Wallace's handiwork.

The woodpecker blushed. "Just a little something to remember me by." And he turned to leave.

"Wait!" said the bears. "You can't go!"

Wallace stopped, unsure of what the bears meant.

"Everyone needs a handyman to fix things up and make them beautiful," explained Mops. "Even in the Grumpy Woods!"

"Helping out is the perfect way to get neighbors to love you!" cheered the bears.

"Yeah. You can be our super

SUPER!"

said the littlest bear.

"Really? I can stay?" asked
Wallace as the bears all surrounded
him in a big bear hug. "HOORAY!
Wait. What's a super?"

CHAPTER FIVE

The bears explained that a super
was simply a supervisor who made
sure everything was shipshape
around the neighborhood and
that Wallace would be responsible
for repairs around the Grumpy
Woods. Wallace liked the sound

of that. After all, he just wanted to make the other towncritters happy.

So the bears all got right to work transforming Wallace into the super-est super the Grumpy Woods could have. First, a tool belt, a button-down shirt that read WALLY, and a set of keys would help Wallace look the part. The keys

didn't actually open any doors in the Grumpy Woods. They were, in reality, just spoons. But the littlest bear insisted that the jingling noise was essential to the uniform.

Next, the bears provided Wallace with a map that showed every residence in the Grumpy Woods,

with each home clearly labeled.
That way, even those hidden *I want
to be left alone* homes—like Bernice
Bunny's—could be easily located.

And last, every handyman needs
a to-do list. So the bears wrote
down tasks for Wallace. Each task
was meant to fix and beautify the
Grumpy Woods, which would, in

theory, make every townscritter
fall in love with Wallace. Super
happily ever after.

"Here. In case you get hungry,"
said Shades, handing Wallace
a metal lunch box. "There are
doughnuts inside. There's even a
jelly one!"

With that, Wallace was off.

As he was finishing his first
job, high up in the trees, Wallace
noticed he wasn't alone. Someone
below was frantically humming her
favorite cleaning-up tune.

It was Dawn Fawn.

"Well, hello there," said Wallace,
flying down to introduce himself.
"I'm the new super of the Grumpy
Woods, and I—"

Dawn came in close. She
sniffed Wallace. She nudged his

key-spoons with her nose. She then dusted his head off with her short little tail.

"I need my dust bunny," she squealed, and trotted off into the brush.

"Cute. She wants to help," Wallace chuckled. But his chuckling was soon interrupted.

"WHOOOOOO are you?" said a pair of angry yellow eyes peeking out from the dense branches. It was Opal Owl, who was rarely seen in the Grumpy Woods. She liked it that way.

"Howdy-doody," said Wallace. "I'm Wallace, the new super of the Grumpy Woods, and I—"

"What did you dooOOOO to my roooOOOOof?"

"Oh that." Wallace blushed. "A little handiwork is all, ma'am. No need to pay me. Just being neighborly."

The yellow eyes only squinted and waited for a better answer.

"It's a sunroof," said Wallace. "The bears thought you might want to let some light into your life."

"I'M NOCTURNAL!" screeched Opal. "I like it dark."

"Maybe a moon-roof, then? I was only trying to help," said Wallace, hanging his head.

"WhoOOOOooo *asked* you toOOOOooo?" she screeched. Wallace was pretty sure her head spun completely around before he lost her in the bright sunlight.

Better luck with the next job, thought Wallace, scanning his list. Next stop was Bernice Bunny's house and then on to City Hall.

CHAPTER SIX

At City Hall, Mayor Quill had just
sat down to nurse his headache
and have his midday bowl of
leaves and berries when someone
knocked on the door.

Knock knock.

"By order of Mayoral Decree four-two-seven—" declared Quill.

Bernice Bunny barged in, and she was hopping mad.

"MY BOOK HAS HOLES!" she announced.

"I tried to stop her, sir," said Humphrey, who followed close behind. "I told her that *now* is no time for a book club meeting."

All day and night, Bernice Bunny's twitchy nose was stuck in a book—which meant the only time she stopped to say anything was

to either shush loud townscritters

or try to discuss her latest read.

So most of the Grumpy Woods
residents left her alone, not
wanting to engage in an unwanted
book club discussion.

"HOLES!" she declared once
again.

"So many books these days have
holes," dismissed Humphrey.

"Precisely," agreed Mayor Quill.

"There's a term for it. What are
they called?"

"Plot holes, sir."

"Right, Humphrey. Plot holes."

"In fact," continued Quill,
"it always bothered me that
everything turns back to its
original form at midnight *except*
Cinderella's shoe. I mean, wouldn't

that have disappeared or become
some boring slipper or something?"

"Brilliant, sir," agreed Humphrey.
"I never thought of that."

"No, no, NO!" yelled Bernice. "A
real, live hole!" Bernice held up
her book and then stuck her ear
through the gaping hole and waved
at Humphrey and Quill.

She went on to explain that
every book in the south branch
of her library—which is literally
the southernmost branch in a

low-lying bush, but don't tell her
that—had been destroyed by
similar holes.

"My dear Bernice," said the
mayor, putting his prickly arm
around her shoulders and guiding
her slowly to the door, "book
vandalism is quite a shame.

We will put it on the agenda for the next town meeting. Now, if you wouldn't mind . . . I am quite busy with *official* mayor business."

Squirrelly Sam, the Grumpy Woods' nosy forest gossip, suddenly appeared, scrambling down from the branches.

"Excuse me, Mr. Mayor.
You didn't hear this from me,
but someone seems to have
turned your City Hall sign into
Swiss cheese. There are holes
everywhere!"

Mayor Quill stomped his foot. He shook from head to toe, and just before he exploded, Humphrey rolled into a defensive ball.

Quills shot out everywhere.
One narrowly missed Sam's tail.
Another soared straight through
the hole in Bernice's book.

Thankfully, she had already pulled her ear out of it.

Humphrey peeked from behind his clipboard.

"Hole in one, sir."

CHAPTER SEVEN

The sign that distinguished Mayor
Quill's City Hall from all the other
upturned logs in the area looked
like a grandma's doily collection.
The once-official-looking marker
was covered in swirly scrolls, and
several of the letters spelling out

CITY HALL were lost in an intricate
pattern. It was actually quite
elegant—unless you were grumpy.

"Preposterous!" proclaimed Quill.

"'C-blank-blank-Y blank-A-L-blank,'" spelled Humphrey. "It looks like a puzzle on a game show."

"'COZY BALL'?" guessed Bernice.

"'CLAY WALK'?" guessed Humphrey.

"I'd like to buy a vowel," said Sam.

"NO ONE IS BUYING ANY VOWELS!" The spines on Mayor Quill's brow quivered, predicting

a storm. Just then, the ground
hissed.

"Newsssss from the front linessss.
Ssssomeone needsssss to buy a
new fence." It was Sherry Snake,
the self-proclaimed sheriff of the
Grumpy Woods.

"Why? What happened to my—

I mean, *our* fence, Sherry?" asked
Humphrey.

"Come on and sssssee for
yoursssselvessss," said Sherry.

The group paraded toward the
Grumpy Woods border, noticing
holes in every tree along the way.
It was as if they were in a life-sized

connect-the-dots game. And sure
enough, the holes led them straight
to the Grumpy Fence and the twigs
on top.

"It looks polka-dotted," said
Squirrelly Sam, sniffing at a larger
hole in the twigs. He could see
right through to the other side.

"I thought you were patrolling
day and night, Sherry! How could
this happen?" yelled Humphrey.

"That's *ssssheriff* to you, and yessss, I was patrolling. But thissss didn't happen on my watch! *Sssssomeone elsssse* was in charge!" She spit toward Sam.

"Me?" said Sam. "I told you I needed a break in the middle of the day for nut collecting and storage. I felt a chill in the air and I panicked, and I thought the winter was coming early and—"

"SILENCE!" said Quill. "This is vandalism! And vandalism such as this will not be tolerated in the Grumpy Woods!"

"Well said, sir. The culprit or *culprits* will be punished," said Humphrey.

"But who would do such a thing?" asked Bernice.

"Well, you didn't hear it from me," started Sam, "but everything is covered in holes. And what else has holes? Doughnuts. And who loves doughnuts?"

"The Ssssuper Happy Party Bearsssss," answered Sherry.

Everyone gasped.

"Makes perfect sense," said Mayor Quill.

But before Mayor Quill could issue a warrant for the arrest of the Super Happy Party Bears, a frantic humming to a familiar cleaning-up tune came up along the wall toward the group. Dawn Fawn was feverishly sweeping up dust. It seemed that whoever had drilled all those holes into the Grumpy Fence had caused quite a mess.

"*Dirty bird! Dirty bird! Dirty bird!*"

Dawn sang on repeat.

Then
Dawn caught
a glimpse of
Bernice and
shrieked, "I
NEED MY DUST
BUNNY!" Before
Bernice could

103

react, Dawn scooped up the bunny with her mouth and started using Bernice's cottontail to tidy up the hills of dust.

"*Eeek!*" screamed Bernice. "Help me!"

"Whatever is going on here?" asked Mayor Quill. "Who is this 'dirty bird' you sing of?"

Dawn's simple description of a woodpecker was enough for Humphrey to know *exactly* who was to blame.

"I'll call a town meeting," said Humphrey.

"Sssshall I go make an arresssst?" asked Sheriff Sherry.

"Knock yourself out," said Quill.

CHAPTER EIGHT

Wallace Woodpecker was very
tired by the time he returned
to the Party Patch. His eyelids
drooped, and he was dragging his
wings. The bears were eager to
find out how his day had gone.

Wallace dropped his lunch box at the door and sighed.

"Well?" asked Mops.

"How was it being the super today?" asked Shades.

"I don't know," said Wallace. "I'm not sure they will like what I did."

"What do you mean?" asked Jigs.

"Of course they will!" She gave her maracas an enthusiastic shake.

"I can almost hear the love now," said the littlest bear.

The littlest bear was right. There was some sort of noise in the distance, but it wasn't love. It was a mob of angry critters, and it was marching straight up the flower-lined path.

All the Grumpy Woods townscritters soon arrived on

the bears' doorstep, even Opal
Owl, who was, of course, wide
awake and had spotted the pack
as they passed her tree. She gladly
abandoned her jigsaw puzzle, put
on her darkest
sunglasses, and
tagged along.

"Come out with your pawsssss up!" instructed Sheriff Sherry, now taking on a very official role.

The bears thought Sherry just wanted them all to *wave their paws in the air like they just don't care* and got very excited.

"See, Wally! They love you!" cheered the bears. And they all burst out the door to join the We Love Wallace celebration.

"IT'S SUPER HAPPY PARTY TIME! SUPER HAPPY PARTY TIME!"

Slide to the right.

Hop to the left.

Shimmy,   shimmy, shake.

Strike a pose.

"Where's Wallace Woodpecker?"
asked Humphrey.

"Wallace!" the bears called into
the Party Patch. "Your fans are
looking for you!"

Wallace bashfully stepped outside.

"You ruined my tree AND my
sleep!" screeched Opal Owl.

"I said I was sorry," replied
Wallace.

"You made holes in all of my
books!" accused Bernice Bunny.

"I was exterminating the
bookworms," explained Wallace.

"You made a mockery of City
Hall!" yelled Mayor Quill.

"I was decorating and got carried away," said Wallace, holding back tears. "I thought maybe a nice pattern would look very classy and official!"

"YOU DESTROYED MY GRUMPY FENCE!" screamed Humphrey.

Everyone froze, then looked at Humphrey.

"*OUR* GRUMPY FENCE!" Humphrey corrected himself.

"I made it so Sherry could see through it, and patrol on *both* sides of the wall at once," Wallace said, and burst into tears. "It's no use. I'm not super. I'm a failure!"

Wallace took off his tool belt and his jingly spoons and flew up into the tree.

"Come down here this instant," said Mayor Quill. "We're not through with you!"

Wallace flew even higher, bumping into one of the Super

Happy Party Bears' mailboxes,
which fell to the ground with a
bang. Out spilled one envelope.

"WE'VE GOT MAIL!" cheered the

bears.

"It's from the beavers!" said the

littlest bear as he tore it open.

"Ooh! Is it a
postcard from
their cruise?"
asked Mops.

"What's this word here? 'Suing'?" asked the littlest bear.

"It's supposed to be 'seeing.' It's a typo," explained Bubs as he blew bubbles in the corner. "It says they will be *seeing* us."

Dear Super Happy Annoying Bears,

We will be suing you.

Truly,
The Beavers

The Bears
Party Patch
Grumpy Woods

"Here's a photograph of their houseboat," said the littlest bear as he passed it around.

Everyone admired the houseboat—even the townscritters.

"It's a little plain, though," said Jigs. "I bet Wallace could do some fine woodworking for them."

"THAT'S IT!" cheered the bears.

"The beavers LOVE fine art and furnishings," said Mops. "Wallace could do woodworking for the beavers!"

Wallace drifted back down to the ground. "You think they would like my work?"

Mayor Quill immediately joined in. "Of course, Wallace. Opportunity knocks! Answer that door!"

The other townscritters caught on quickly. They were very eager to send Wallace off on this adventure, so they changed their tune and started handing out compliments.

"Have yoooou seen the be-yoooo-tiful sunroooof Wallace made me?" Opal Owl asked the others. "It's cured my daytime drowsiness."

Everyone applauded.

"Wallace got rid of every bookworm in my library while also getting rid of all the boring parts in my books," boasted Bernice.

Humphrey patted Wallace on the back.

"And the City Hall sign!" added
Mayor Quill. "Not only is it super
fancy, but the misplaced letters
also add a layer of mystery to the
place."

"Thank you," said Wallace. "I don't know what to say. I really appreciate your belief in me."

Mayor Quill placed his prickly arm around Wallace's shoulders and guided him toward the

flower-lined path. "So I guess this is good-bye, then, Wallace."

"Wait!" said the littlest bear. "Aren't you forgetting something?"

"It's time for a SUPER HAPPY GOING-AWAY PARTY!" cheered the bears.

CHAPTER NINE

The bears threw a Going-Away
Party fit for the super-est of supers,
complete with doughnuts and
dancercise. All the townscritters
were there. They were so pleased
that the noise was going to stop
that they even partied a
little bit themselves.

128

Ziggy played guitar. Well, it wasn't really a guitar. More like a few rubber bands stretched across a beautifully carved piece of wood—courtesy of Wallace.

The Super Happy Party Band played their signature dance remix of "If You're Happy and You Know It." Dawn Fawn even joined in and sang a few bars.

Sherry Snake and Flips started
a rousing game of doughnut
ringtoss. Sherry didn't mind having
doughnuts tossed at her. She loved
sinking her teeth into each one that
found its way around her neck.

And Humphrey shared stories
of his life in City Hall. Actually,
Bubs was the only one listening. He
calmly blew his party bubbles as
Humphrey went on and on.

It was a good time for all. But

soon it was time for good-bye and to send Wallace off in search of an exciting career as a woodworker.

All the bears gave Wallace a hug. The woodpecker spread his wings out and said, "Thank you

all so much! You have helped me find what I was meant to do! You are my best friends!" Then Wallace grabbed his knapsack and headed down the flower-lined path.

"Send us a postcard," said the littlest bear.

"IT'S SUPER SUPER WALLY TIME! SUPER SUPER WALLY TIME!" cheered the bears, and they did their Super Happy Party Dance. And you know what?

The townscritters danced, too.
They were feeling just a *little less*
grumpy. THE END.

ABOUT THE AUTHOR

In previous chapters, Marcie Colleen
has been a teacher, an actress, and
a nanny, but now she spends her
days writing children's books! She
lives in her very own Party Patch,
Headquarters of Fun, with her husband
and their mischievous sock monkey
in San Diego, California. Occasionally,
there are even doughnuts. This is her
first chapter book series.

Don't Miss the other
SUPER HAPPY PARTY BEARS
BOOKS

SUPER HAPPY PARTY BEARS

GNAWING AROUND

MARCIE COLLEEN